GALAXY ZACK

ZACK

THE PREHISTORIC PLANET

By Ray O'Ryan

Illustrated by Colin Jack

LITTLE SIMON

New York   London   Toronto   Sydney   New Delhi

LITTLE SIMON

An imprint of Simon & Schuster Children's Publishing Division 1230 Avenue of the Americas, New York, New York 10020 Copyright © 2013 by Simon & Schuster, Inc. All rights reserved, including the right of reproduction in whole or in part in any form. LITTLE SIMON is a registered trademark of Simon & Schuster, Inc., and associated colophon is a trademark of Simon & Schuster, Inc. For information about special discounts for bulk purchases, please contact Simon & Schuster Special Sales at 1-866-506-1949 or business@simonandschuster.com. The Simon & Schuster Speakers Bureau can bring authors to your live event. For more information or to book an event contact the Simon & Schuster Speakers Bureau at 1-866-248-3049 or visit our website at www.simonspeakers.com. Designed by Ciara Gay. Manufactured in the United States of America 0513 FFG First Edition 1 2 3 4 5 6 7 8 9 10 Library of Congress Cataloging-in-Publication Data O'Ryan, Ray. The Prehistoric Planet / by Ray O'Ryan ; illustrated by Colin Jack. — First edition. pages cm (Galaxy Zack ; 3) Summary: Zack and his father are invited to join the Nebulon Navigators as they set out to return a lost baby pterosaur to the Prehistoric Planet, where Zack sees animals and plants he had only read about in books.
ISBN 978-1-4424-6715-6 (pbk.)
ISBN 978-1-4424-6716-3 (hardcover)
ISBN 978-1-4424-6717-0 (ebook) [1. Science fiction. 2. Planets—Fiction. 3. Pterosaurs—Fiction. 4. Animals—Infancy—Fiction. 5. Dinosaurs—Fiction.] I. Title. PZ7.O7843Pre 2013 [Fic]—dc23 2013003347

CONTENTS

Chapter 1

Run for Your Life!

Zack Nelson ran through a jungle. Every tree he saw looked different. They were nothing like the trees that he knew on Earth. They were also not like any tree he had seen so far on his new home planet, Nebulon.

In the distance Zack saw a huge

1

waterfall. It rose hundreds of feet into the air. The water crashed into a lake below, making a sound like thunder.

Zack felt confused as he ran along a path.

Omph!

Zack tripped over a large white rock and landed on his

stomach. As he picked himself back up he heard a *ka-raaaaack!!!*

This noise was followed by a high-pitched screech behind him.

Screeeeeeee!!!

Turning back toward the white rock, Zack discovered that it was not a rock at all. It was a huge egg. A tiny creature stepped out of the egg. It let out another ear-splitting yell.

Screeeeeeee!!!

"I've seen pictures of that animal,"

Zack said to himself.
"It's a baby Tyrannosaurus
rex! They're cute when they're
small."

Suddenly, the ground began to
shake. An earth-shaking roar split the
air.

ROOOAAAARRRRR!

Zack looked up and saw a huge

Tyrannosaurus rex rumbling toward him.

"YAAAAA!" he shouted, running in terror. "They're not so cute when they're big!"

Zack ran through the jungle, crashing through branches and leaves. He looked back over his shoulder and saw the giant dinosaur catching up to him.

That's when he began to hear familiar music.

"Wait a minute," he said. "I know that song. It's 'Rockin' Round the Stars' by Retro Rocket. But how can it be playing here in this jungle?"

The music grew louder and louder. The dinosaur got closer and closer.

"Master Just Zack," said a very familiar voice. "It is time to get ready for school."

"Ira?" Zack asked.

Zack's eyes popped open. He saw that he was not in a jungle. He was in his bed, sweating from his nightmare.

Ira, the Nelson family's Indoor

Robotic Assistant, was waking Zack up. He did this every morning by playing Zack's favorite song. Zack bolted from his bed, rubbed the sleep from his eyes, and thought, *I've GOT to explore the Prehistoric Planet!*

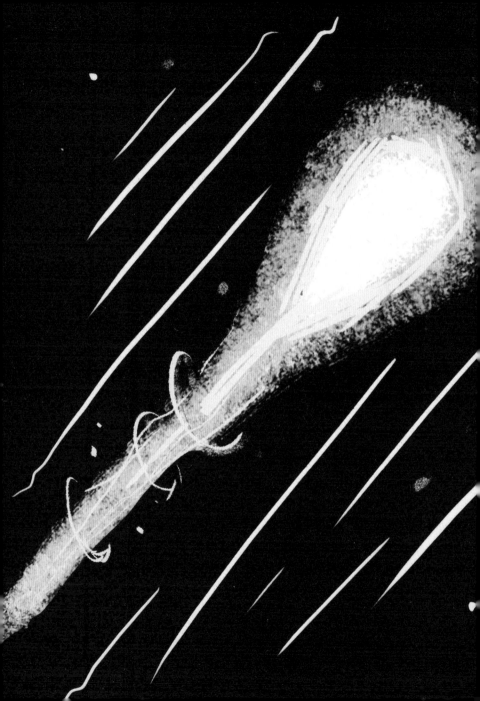

Chapter 2

Pterosaur Troubles

At breakfast the next morning Zack couldn't stop thinking about the real-life dinosaur that was right there on Nebulon. The week before, Zack had seen something streaking through the sky. He looked through his überzoom telescope and was amazed to see a

Extinct Dinosaur Found!

creature flying through the air above Nebulon.

When the creature landed, it turned out to be a baby pterosaur—a dinosaur that had been extinct on Earth for hundreds of millions of years! News of the pterosaur spread through z-mail blasts and sonic cell news

OH, BABY! Pterosaur Hits Nebulon

reports. Soon everyone on Nebulon and even throughout the entire galaxy knew about the creature.

Wow! Check Out This Dino!

Zack's dad, Otto Nelson, sat at the breakfast table reading the *Nebulon News*. This was the planet's online holographic newspaper. Lifelike 3-D images of the dinosaur flapping its wings in a cage jumped from the screen of his tablet reader.

"I studied pterosaurs on Earth," explained Zack. "I learned how to pronounce their name! You say it like 'TER-oh-sore.' And I learned that they look like giant birds. They have long pointy beaks. And the backs of their heads come to a point. Their wings are bigger than their skinny bodies. And they have long narrow tails."

"You do know a lot about pterosaurs, Zack," said Dad. "At least this one is safe, and the top scientists on Nebulon are taking good care of him. They're trying to build him a bigger cage for him to fly in."

"The poor thing," said Zack's mom, Shelly Nelson. "How long do you think it'll take them to find its home planet?"

"No one knows for sure, honey," Dad said. "The scientists are looking as hard as they can for the Prehistoric Planet, where the pterosaur came from. It could be days, weeks, even

years before they find the planet."

"Years?" asked Zack. "I hope it doesn't take that long."

"Poor little guy . . ."

". . . he must be . . ."

". . . so scared," said Charlotte and Cathy, Zack's twin sisters.

"Everyone at Nebulonics is working

very hard to find his home," said Dad.

Nebulonics was where Zack's dad worked. It was the best electronics research company on the planet. Nebulonics was always inventing new things to help make life easier.

"We're building an ultra-shuttle that can safely and quickly make the trip to the Prehistoric Planet. We're going

to take the poor fella home."

"That's pretty grape," said Zack. In the few months he had lived on Nebulon, Zack had gotten comfortable using the word "grape" instead of "cool."

"You bet, Captain," Dad said, getting up from the table. "Well, time for work. I'll see you all tonight."

Captain! Zack thought. "Captain" was what Zack's dad liked to call him.

But this time it made Zack imagine himself at the controls of the ultra-shuttle. He was piloting the space ship, taking the pterosaur back home.

"Hey, that reminds me," said Dad just before he reached the front door. "Tomorrow is Bring Your Child to Work Day on Earth. I asked my boss, Fred Stevens, if I could bring you to work, Zack. And even though Nebulites have

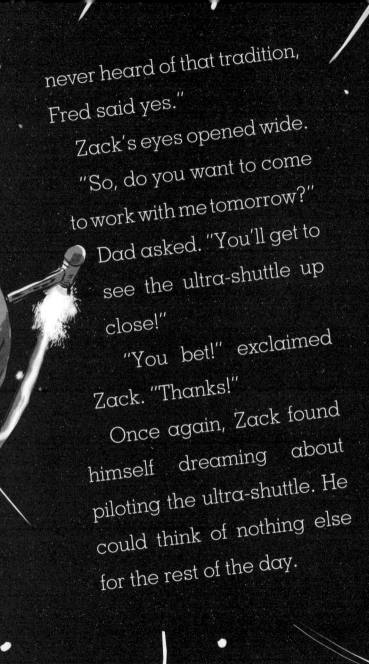

never heard of that tradition,
Fred said yes."

Zack's eyes opened wide.
"So, do you want to come
to work with me tomorrow?"
Dad asked. "You'll get to
see the ultra-shuttle up
close!"

"You bet!" exclaimed
Zack. "Thanks!"

Once again, Zack found
himself dreaming about
piloting the ultra-shuttle. He
could think of nothing else
for the rest of the day.

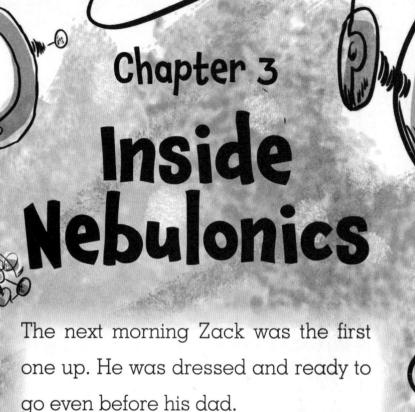

Chapter 3
Inside Nebulonics

The next morning Zack was the first one up. He was dressed and ready to go even before his dad.

"All set, Zack?" asked Dad.

"Yup! I'm taking my new camtram so I can take pictures of all the grape stuff at Nebulonics," Zack replied,

holding up his handheld device.

Zack and his dad slipped into the shiny red Nebulonics car. They sped through the sky above Creston City.

A few minutes later they landed in the conveyor lot at Nebulonics.

"This is it!" Dad said excitedly.

Zack could tell that his dad was really happy to have him there.

As soon as they stepped out of the car, a large robotic arm sprung out from a conveyor belt. It lifted the car onto the moving belt. Then the car disappeared into a storage slot where it would stay until Dad needed it at the end of the day.

Zack stepped into the Nebulonics building. He couldn't believe his eyes!

Everywhere he looked, people were busy putting things together. Some were building machines that moved on their own. Others wired up complex computer circuits.

This place is cool! Dad is lucky to have a job like this, Zack thought as he looked around.

Dad's boss, Fred Stevens, came over to welcome them.

"Glad you are here, Zack," said Fred. "Feel free to look around."

"Thank you, Mr. Stevens!" Zack replied.

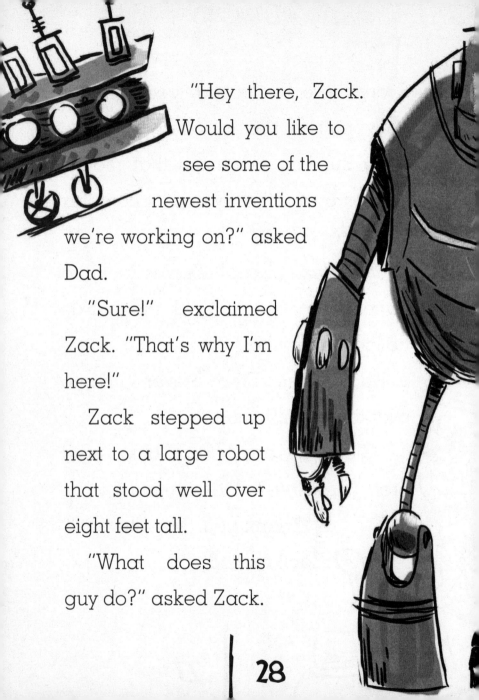

"Hey there, Zack. Would you like to see some of the newest inventions we're working on?" asked Dad.

"Sure!" exclaimed Zack. "That's why I'm here!"

Zack stepped up next to a large robot that stood well over eight feet tall.

"What does this guy do?" asked Zack.

"It's the latest model of galactic blast robot," explained Dad. "They'll be on the field next season. They're twice as fast as the current players."

"Wow!" Zack cried. "I can't wait to go to a galactic blast game next season!"

Zack couldn't be happier. He used his camtram to take photos and movies of all the amazing gadgets.

They came around a corner and Zack stopped in his tracks. There stood the coolest bicycle ever made.

"It's the Torkus Magnus!" Zack exclaimed. "I saw Seth Stevens riding one!"

Seth was Fred's son. He was also the school bully, and the only kid who had a Torkus Magnus bike.

"Why don't I take a picture of you on the bike?" asked Dad.

"Yeah!" Zack cried, handing his dad the camtram. He climbed onto the bike, which was mounted on a stand.

"Here I am riding the Torkus Magnus!" Zack said into the camtram. He pressed the buttons and turned the handlebars.

Zack didn't want to get off. Even though the bike wasn't going any-where, he loved the idea of riding it.

"Okay, c'mon, Zack," Dad said after a couple of minutes. "There's a lot more to see."

Chapter 4
Ultra Grape!

The tour continued. In each room Zack saw another cool gadget.

"I think you'll really like this," Dad said. He pointed to a telescope that looked a lot like the überzoom galactic telescope Zack had in his room.

"We call this the Galactic Uplink,"

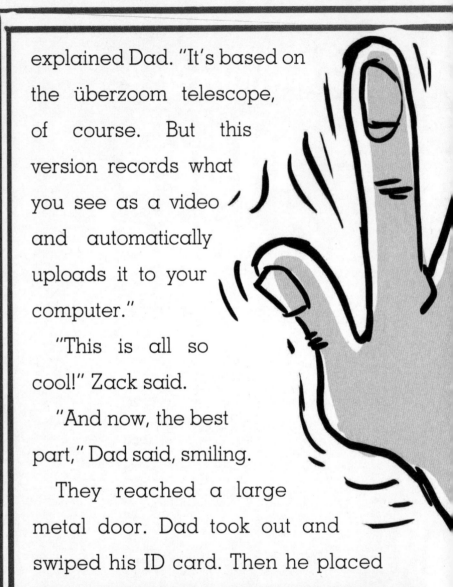

explained Dad. "It's based on the überzoom telescope, of course. But this version records what you see as a video and automatically uploads it to your computer."

"This is all so cool!" Zack said.

"And now, the best part," Dad said, smiling.

They reached a large metal door. Dad took out and swiped his ID card. Then he placed his hand on a screen. The screen flashed green.

"Your turn," said Dad.

Zack put his hand up on the screen. It flashed again.

"Otto Nelson and one guest," a voice from the screen said. "You are cleared to enter."

The door slid open and they walked into a large room with a high ceiling. In the center of the room sat the ultra-shuttle.

"WHOA!" Zack exclaimed. "That's what you're building to take the pterosaur home!"

"Exactly," replied Dad. "Everyone here at Nebulonics has been working on it ever since the pterosaur landed on Nebulon. It's almost ready."

Zack turned on his camtram and took video of the shuttle from all angles.

Just then the door to the shuttle room slid open. In rushed Fred Stevens.

"Otto, have you heard the news?" Mr. Stevens asked excitedly.

"What news?" asked Dad.

"It just came across the sonic cell monitor," explained Mr. Stevens. "It looks like the Nebulon Navigators have found the Prehistoric Planet!"

Chapter 5

An Unexpected Trip

That night at dinner all Zack could talk about was the Prehistoric Planet. He had had a great day at Nebulonics, but this amazing discovery was the biggest news of the year.

"A team of scientists used a test model of the new Galactic Uplink telescope," explained Dad. "And the Nebulon Navigators used star charts they had created during their missions exploring the galaxy."

"Like the mission I went on with them to Juno!" Zack said excitedly.

"Exactly," replied Dad. "And their timing couldn't have been better. We'll have the ultra-shuttle ready soon. Then we can bring the pterosaur home."

At that moment Dad's hyperphone began to buzz.

"Excuse me," he said, pulling it from his pocket. "It's from Fred."

"He doesn't usually z-mail you at home," Zack's mom pointed out.

"It must . . ."

". . . be very . . ."

". . . important,"
Charlotte and
Cathy added.

"You said it, girls!" Dad exclaimed
after he read the z-mail. "Nebulonics
wants me to go on the mission to the
Prehistoric Planet!"

"That is so grape, Dad!" said Zack.

"It sure is! They want an engineer
on board to make sure that everything
on the ultra-shuttle runs smoothly.
I'm going with the scientists and the

Nebulon Navigators to take the lost pterosaur home!"

"Wow!" cried Zack. "Can I go with you? Please, Dad? Please, please, please? You know how much I love planet hopping. And I've already been on one mission with the Nebulon Navigators. And I think that dinosaurs are super-cool!"

"Uh . . . I don't know, Captain," said Dad. "I'll talk with Fred tomorrow."

After dinner, Zack took his dog, Luna, for a walk. He did this every evening. He loved talking to Luna even though she couldn't talk back. She was a good listener.

"Dad is going to take that dinosaur

home, Luna," Zack said as Luna trotted along beside him. "And guess what?"

Luna looked up at him and tilted her head. She looked as if she were waiting for the answer.

"*I* may get to go too!"

Yip! Yip! Luna barked.

"Isn't that great?!" said Zack.

That night Zack could hardly sleep. His mind was filled with nothing but dinosaurs. He imagined the homepage of the *Nebulon News* with the headline: EARTH BOY AND NAVIGATORS SAVE BABY DINOSAUR! Next to the headline there would be a photo of Zack with the pterosaur and a group of Nebulon Navigators.

When Zack finally fell asleep, he again dreamed about running through a jungle filled with dinosaurs.

Chapter 6

Zack Nelson, Daydreamer

The next day at school Zack sat in Ms. Rudolph's class. He was still daydreaming about the Prehistoric Planet. He could see himself with the Nebulon Navigators, watching as the baby pterosaur was reunited with its mother.

A distant voice sounded in the jungle.

"Zack?" the voice seemed to be saying.

Then it got a bit louder. "Zack!"

Then it was *really* loud. "ZACK NELSON! Please pay attention!"

Zack snapped out of his daydream to find Ms. Rudolph standing over him.

"I asked you a question about the second age of Nebulon history," said Ms. Rudolph.

"I'm sorry, Ms. Rudolph. I'll pay attention. I promise."

During lunch Zack told his friend Drake Tucker all about the pterosaur, Nebulonics, and how he might be able to go on the trip.

"How can I think about school when I may be rocketing to the Prehistoric Planet?" asked Zack. "I can't think about anything else—not even this super-yummy galactic patty."

Drake was excited for his friend. "That would be so grape!" said Drake. He took a sip of his cosmic cooler. "What do you think that planet is like?"

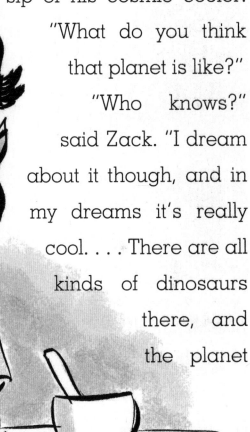

"Who knows?" said Zack. "I dream about it though, and in my dreams it's really cool. . . . There are all kinds of dinosaurs there, and the planet

is filled with waterfalls and strange trees."

"Do you know when you would leave?" Drake asked.

"No," said Zack, thinking. "The ultra-shuttle isn't ready yet."

Just then Seth Stevens walked by. He was telling his friends about the baby pterosaur. "Yeah, I saw him up close. He is kind of wimpy. They are taking him home in two weeks."

Two weeks? wondered Zack. *How will I be able to wait two weeks?*

After what seemed like the longest day ever, school finally ended. Zack rushed home. He paced back and forth in his room, hoping his hyperphone would ring.

Zack stared at his

hyperphone as if that might force it to ring. Then he paced some more.

What could be keeping him? Zack wondered.

Suddenly his hyperphone rang. *This is it!* Zack answered it.

"Hey, Dad," he said nervously.

"Hi, Captain," Dad replied. "So,

what are you doing the day after tomorrow?"

Zack thought for a second. Two days from now was Sunday.

"Do you think you can come with me to the Prehistoric Planet?" Dad asked.

Zack almost jumped out of his skin. "Mr. Stevens said yes?" cried Zack.

"He sure did!" Dad replied.

"But I didn't think the ultra-shuttle would be ready so fast," Zack explained.

"We're putting the finishing touches on it tomorrow. Then the day after it'll blast off to the Prehistoric Planet!

"And *I'm* coming with you!" Zack exclaimed. "YIPPEE WAH-WAH!"

Chapter 7

Ready to Fly!

Zack got up early on Sunday. He was so excited—he was ready to go two hours before his dad was even awake! As Luna watched, Zack charged up his camtram. He made sure all the settings were correct. He didn't want to miss this once-in-a-lifetime chance

to get pictures of a real live dinosaur on its home planet.

"Dinosaurs lived even before there were dogs," Zack said to Luna.

Yip! Yip! barked Luna.

"I wish I could take you with me on this trip," said Zack. "But it's a people-only journey. Except, of course, for the pterosaur we're taking home."

Urrr—urrr, Luna

whined, as if she knew she couldn't go.

Zack set the focus on his camtram to the setting that made the images look extra-sharp. Then he put it into his carry bag and waited.

Time passed super-slowly.

Finally, Dad's voice rang out from the commu-link speaker in the wall of Zack's bedroom. "Ready to fly, Captain?"

"You bet!" Zack yelled back.

He dashed into the elevator with Luna right behind him. It traveled sideways through the house and arrived at the garage. Dad was waiting, along with Mom, Cathy, and Charlotte.

"Permission to go to the Prehistoric Planet, Captain?" asked Dad, smiling.

"Permission granted, Mr. Nelson," Zack joked back at his dad.

"Now have a safe trip, you two explorers," said Mom.

"And take . . ."

". . . that baby dinosaur . . ."

". . . home to its mother," added Cathy and Charlotte.

Dad climbed into his red Nebulonics car. He left the door open for Zack.

"Forget something?" Dad asked.

"Oh wow!" exclaimed Zack. "I'm so excited, I almost forgot my camtram. I'll be right back."

Zack ran into the house, picked up his carry bag, and raced back out to the car. He climbed in and closed the door behind him.

"What are you waiting for, Dad?" asked Zack. "We've got a dinosaur to

take home!"

Dad smiled and launched the car into the sky. A few minutes later they arrived at Nebulonics. Zack and his dad entered the huge building and headed to the shuttle bay. There, Zack met the other members of the crew.

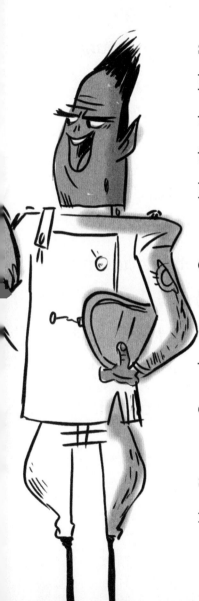

"Everyone, this is my son, Zack Nelson," Dad began. "He'll be joining us on the mission. Zack, this is Captain Zorflane. He'll be our pilot."

"Good to have you aboard, Zack," Captain Zorflane said.

"And this is Raxite Yakko, our copilot," Dad continued.

"Hi, Zack. Welcome," said a tall Nebulite. Both men were wearing the uniform of the Nebulon Navigators. "I remember you. You are the young man who found that giant gemmite on Juno."

"Yes, sir," Zack said proudly. "I'm a new member of the Sprockets Academy Explorers Club."

It's hard to believe I'm going on another trip with the Nebulon Navigators! Zack thought.

Chapter 8

A Stowaway

Suddenly the hatch to the ultra-shuttle opened.

WHOOOSH!

This is so grape!

Then a large shuttle-bay door slid open. In rolled a cage on wheels. Inside the cage sat the most amazing

creature Zack had ever seen.

Zack's jaw dropped open. He pointed at the creature.

"Wow!" said Zack. "A real live dinosaur from the past."

"Not from the past, Zack," explained Captain Zorflane. "This pterosaur is right here, right now. And I think it

is now ready to go home."

The pterosaur spread its wings and opened its mouth wide.

Ka-caaaaw! Ka-caaaaw!

The dinosaur's cry echoed around the shuttle bay.

"Captain Zorflane, I think you're right!" said Zack, smiling.

"Then what are we waiting for?" asked Dad. "Let's go!"

Zack and the rest of the crew climbed on board. Zack strapped himself into his seat. Then the pterosaur's cage was loaded onto the ship. The ultra-shuttle's hatch closed.

"Three . . . two . . . one . . . BLAST OFF!"

The ultra-shuttle's

engines roared. Within a few seconds Zack was in space. He immediately felt right at home.

The ultra-shuttle was almost twenty times as big as the Nelson family's space cruiser. That ship had carried the family from Earth to their new home on Nebulon.

This spacecraft had seats for fifty passengers. It also had a huge cargo area. That's where the pterosaur's cage sat.

I love space travel! thought Zack. He looked out the window as they whizzed by stars and planets.

Ka-caaaaw! Ka-caaaaw!

The pterosaur's cry filled the ship.

"It's okay," Zack called out. "We're taking you home."

Zack looked over at the cage. The scared pterosaur spread its huge

wings and opened its long beak.

Ka-caaaaw! Ka-caaaaw! it cried again.

Urrr—urrr, came a whining moan.

"Wait a minute," said Zack. "What's that?"

Urrr—urrr.

"That's not the pterosaur. . . . That sounds like Luna!"

Just then Luna crawled out from under Zack's seat.

"What are you doing here, girl?"

Yip! Yip! Luna barked.

"How in the world did she end up on board the ultra-shuttle?" Dad asked.

Zack thought for a moment.

"Well, the door to the Nebulonics car was open while I ran back into the house to get my camtram," Zack recalled. "And then the hatch to the shuttle was open while we were all looking at

84

the pterosaur in the shuttle bay."

"She must have snuck into the car, then snuck on board the ultra-shuttle!" exclaimed Dad.

"Luna, you sneaky girl. You're coming with us after all!" Zack cried.

"I guess you're not the only one who's excited about seeing dinosaurs," Dad said to

Zack. The crew chuckled.

Luna jumped onto Zack's lap. She stared out the window at the stars streaking past.

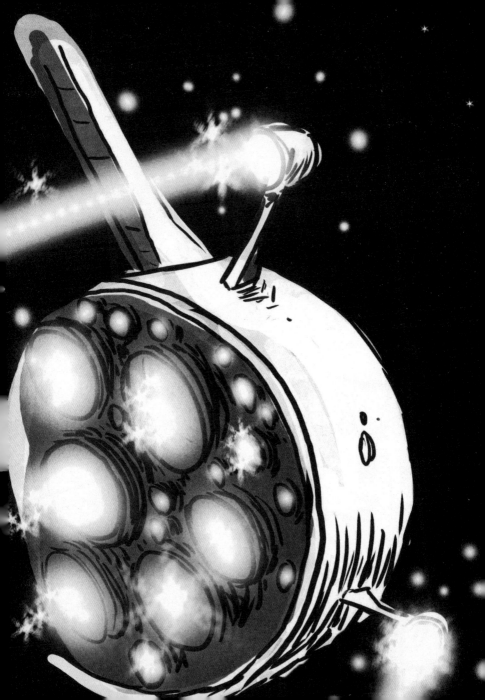

Chapter 9

The Prehistoric Planet

Several hours later the Prehistoric Planet came into view.

"Crew, please prepare for landing," Captain Zorflane announced.

I'm part of the crew, thought Zack. *This is so grape!*

The ship dropped through the

clouds. Zack watched as the planet came closer and closer. A few seconds later the ultra-shuttle landed.

The hatch opened with a hiss. Zack and the other members of the crew stepped outside.

A thick jungle spread out in every direction. Tall trees swayed gently in the hot, steamy breeze. Their big, broad leaves waved like fans.

Zack pulled the camtram

from his bag and began recording. "I can't believe it!" cried Zack. "This planet looks exactly like the planet in my dream!"

Suddenly the soft breeze whipped up into a huge gust of wind. The trees began to bend and shake.

"There's some strange weather on this planet," said Zack. "It changes so quickly."

KA-CAAAAW! KA-CAAAAW!

A deafening screech shattered the silence.

"It's the pterosaur!" cried Zack. But when he looked around, he didn't see the pterosaur.

"We have not taken the pterosaur out of the ship yet," said one of the Nebulon Navigators.

Then a much softer cry came from inside the ultra-shuttle.

Ka-caaaaw! Ka-caaaaw!

It sounded to Zack like the baby pterosaur was trying to answer the louder call.

"We need to get our passenger out of the ship!" shouted Captain Zorflane.

The Nebulon Navigators quickly

rolled the cage out of the shuttle.

Again a blast of wind swept through the jungle. Then came another ear-splitting shriek.

KA-CAAAAW! KA-CAAAAW!

The baby pterosaur in the cage spread its wings and let out a long, sad cry.

Ka-caaaaaaaaaw! Ka-caaaaaaw!

"Open the cage!" shouted Captain Zorflane.

The Nebulon Navigators opened the latch and threw open the cage door.

The pterosaur flapped its wings and took off into the sky.

KA-CAAAAW! KA-CAAAAW! came the loud roar once again.

The baby pterosaur flew off toward the sound of the roar. Luna dashed through the jungle trying to follow

the pterosaur. She crashed through
branches and leaves. Zack and the
crew followed close behind.

*It's weird that this is so much like
my dream*, thought Zack.

When Zack and the others reached
a clearing, the wind picked up again.

KA-CAAAAW! KA-CAAAAW!

This time
the loud roar was
directly overhead.

Zack looked up and saw a pterosaur flapping its wings in the sky. Only
this one was twice as big as the one
they had brought on the shuttle!

Ka-caaaaw! Ka-caaaaw!

The baby pterosaur flew into view. It
screeched happily.

"We did it!" cried Zack. "We brought the baby pterosaur home to its mother!"

The two pterosaurs flew around each other in a circle. Then they flew off over the jungle.

"Let's follow them!" suggested Zack. He pointed his camtram into the air to record the flying dinosaurs.

Zack and the others plunged back into the jungle, following the pterosaurs overhead. As he walked, Zack recorded pictures of trees and plants. Luna walked along beside him sniffing at the ground.

"Hey!" said Zack, stepping up to a plant with many layers. "I recognize this plant. I learned about it in my science

class back on Earth. It's called a horsetail, Luna."

Yip! Yip! Luna barked happily in response.

Glancing overhead, Zack saw the two pterosaurs make a sharp turn.

I wonder where they're going, he thought.

Zack walked along, looking up so he could keep an eye on the pterosaurs.

Suddenly the ground under his feet changed from soft leaves to hard gravel. When he looked down again he was shocked to see that he was at the edge of a cliff!

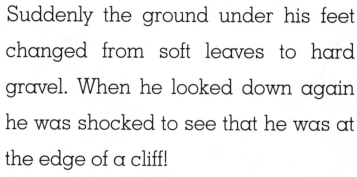

Zack immediately stopped, but he lost his footing. He  started to slip over the edge of the cliff!

Chapter 10

Home—to Nebulon

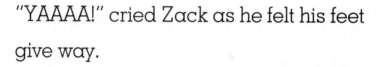

"YAAAA!" cried Zack as he felt his feet give way.

"Zack!" yelled Dad, dashing toward his son.

Luna latched on to Zack's jacket with her teeth. She held him steady long enough for Dad to reach him.

Dad grabbed Zack and pulled him back to safety.

"Be careful, buddy," Dad said to Zack. "Let's all try to get back to Nebulon in one piece!"

"Thanks, Dad. Thanks, Luna," said Zack, scratching her head.

Yip! Yip! Luna barked.

The pterosaurs disappeared into

the distance. Zack gazed across the valley below the cliff.

"Dad! Look at that!" he cried, pointing.

Across the valley he saw a huge waterfall, just like the one from his dream. Only this one was even bigger.

"Wow!" Dad said. "That's the biggest waterfall I've ever seen— on Earth or on Nebulon."

"And look at all the dinosaurs down at the bottom!" exclaimed Zack.

A family of brachiosaurs drank peacefully from the lake at the bottom of the waterfall. Their long necks bent gracefully toward the water.

Beside them, two baby triceratops splashed around in the lake. They gently nudged each other with the three huge horns on their heads.

Suddenly the ground began to shake.

"Are we having an earthquake?" Dad asked.

"No, look!" said Zack, pointing down to a ridge just below.

There, two big Tyrannosaurus rex wrestled with each other. Their size and power made the ground shake.

"Wow! They're huge!" exclaimed Zack. "I studied the Tyrannosaurus rex back on Earth. The name means 'King of the Thunder Lizard.' They're called 'T. rex' for short."

The ground rumbled beneath their feet.

Luna ran to the edge of the cliff. She looked down and barked at the T. rex.

Yip! Yip!

The T. rex looked up. It stared right at Luna.

GRRRRRRRRROOOOAAAARRRR! it growled, then roared at Luna.

The frightened dog jumped up

into Zack's arms and began to whimper.

"Oh! It's okay, girl," Zack said, scratching behind her ear. "I think you should stick to barking at squirrels."

"Okay, everyone," Captain Zorflane announced. "We have completed our mission. It is time to go home."

"I can't wait to get back to Nebulon and tell everyone all about our adventure," Zack told his dad. Then he suddenly realized that, for the first time since he moved from Earth, Zack thought of Nebulon as his home.

Back on the ultra-shuttle Zack settled into his seat. Luna curled up on his lap.

"Three . . . two . . . one . . . BLAST OFF!"

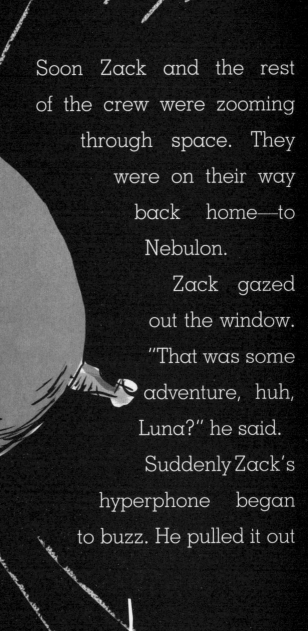

Soon Zack and the rest of the crew were zooming through space. They were on their way back home—to Nebulon.

Zack gazed out the window. "That was some adventure, huh, Luna?" he said.

Suddenly Zack's hyperphone began to buzz. He pulled it out

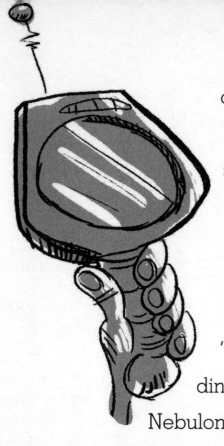

of his carry bag.

"It's Bert," Zack said. "He's calling from Earth."

"Hey, Zack," said Bert over the hyperphone. "I heard that a dinosaur landed on Nebulon. It was all over the news here on Earth. Did you get to see it?"

"Not only did I get to see it," began Zack, "but I was part of the team that brought it back to its home planet—a planet where dinosaurs still live! I'm on the ultra-shuttle that my dad helped design! It's soooooo grape!"

"Okay, first," said Bert, "I'm still going to have to get used to that saying. And second . . . how COOL is that? I wish I was there!"

"Don't worry," said Zack. "I have it

all in my
camtram. I'll
z-mail you the videos
as soon as I get home."

Nebulon *really is
starting to feel like
home,* Zack thought.
Now THAT'S pretty grape!

GALAXY ZACK

ADVENTURE!

HERE'S A SNEAK PEEK!

Zack had dozed off that morning after his alarm played. Breakfast took longer than usual, and his dog, Luna, had insisted on a last-minute walk.

Zack dashed across the wide lobby, and he ran into a round opening in the wall. A door hissed shut and he took

An excerpt from *Monsters in Space!*

off. The clear round elevator looked more like a giant plastic ball. It sped through a tube going sideways. A few seconds later it stopped.

The door whooshed open, and Zack burst into his classroom. Everyone was already in his or her usual seat. Zack ran toward his seat and suddenly stopped in his tracks.

There's someone in my seat! Zack thought.

He looked closely. *No! Not someone, some-THING! A monster!*

A huge purple monster sat in his seat. The monster was at least four

An excerpt from *Monsters in Space!*

times as big as Zack. It was furry with green patches, and it had five eyes. Its pointy ears stuck out from its face.

I've got to save my class before the monster does something terrible, Zack thought. *But how?*

Zack spotted Drake Taylor. Ever since Zack and his family moved from Earth to Nebulon, Drake had been his best new friend. Zack hurried to Drake's side.

"Drake! What is that thing doing here?" Zack whispered, pointing at the monster.

An excerpt from *Monsters in Space!*

The monster yawned. Its mouth was filled with long, sharp teeth.

"What's it going to do to us?"

Drake gave Zack a puzzled look. Before Drake could say anything, their teacher, Ms. Rudolph, stepped into the room.

"Okay, class, let's begin," she said. "Please turn on your edu-screens. Today we are going to continue our study of the second age of Nebulon history."

Zack stared at Ms. Rudolph in disbelief.

An excerpt from *Monsters in Space!*

Doesn't she see it? he wondered. *Isn't she afraid of the monster?*

Ms. Rudolph began her lesson.

Zack looked around at his classmates. They were all paying attention. No one seemed bothered by the fact that a big purple monster was right there in the room.

Zack slipped into an empty seat.

Ms. Rudolph continued the lesson.

What's wrong with everyone? Zack wondered. *Why aren't they scared?*

An excerpt from *Monsters in Space!*